**The General Federation
of Women's Clubs**

This book is a gift from

Dallas Woman's Club
club name

Oregon
state

*in support of GFWC's
commitment
to libraries and literacy*

THE
GIFT STONE

by **Robyn Eversole**

illustrated by **Allen Garns**

ALFRED A. KNOPF NEW YORK

To my dad
—R.E.

For Dude and Thelma
—A.G.

THIS IS A BORZOI BOOK PUBLISHED BY ALFRED A. KNOPF, INC.

Text copyright © 1998 by Robyn Eversole
Illustrations copyright © 1998 by Allen Garns

All rights reserved under International and Pan-American Copyright Conventions.
Published in the United States of America by Alfred A. Knopf, Inc., New York,
and simultaneously in Canada by Random House of Canada Limited, Toronto.
Distributed by Random House, Inc., New York.

www.randomhouse.com/kids/

Library of Congress Cataloging-in-Publication Data
Eversole, Robyn Harbert.
The gift stone / by Robyn Eversole ; illustrated by Allen Garns.
p.   cm.
Summary: Jean, who lives underground in an Australian opal mining town,
finds a precious stone large enough to allow her to move into
a proper house with her grandparents.
ISBN 0-679-88684-2 (trade) — ISBN 0-679-98684-7 (lib. bdg.)
[1. Opal mines and mining—Fiction. 2. Australia—Fiction.
3. Grandparents—Fiction.] I. Garns, Allen, ill. II. Title.
PZ7.E9235Gi   1998
[Fic]—dc21   97-2802

Printed in Singapore
10 9 8 7 6 5 4 3 2 1

2/99

This town is dust and rock
and digging machines and sky.
Come, I'll show you where we live...

…underground.
The walls are rock,
streaked rust-orange and white,
the doorways are rock, the floors, everything
is cool, hard rock.

I didn't always live here.
We used to live in a house with a pointed roof
and windows,
and grass outside, down in South Australia.
But Dad and I came here to Coober Pedy
because of Uncle Peter and Aunt Grace
and the opals.

Opals are rock, too,
but they're special rock
with fire in them, and they're worth money,
which is something we never had much of
back when we had windows.

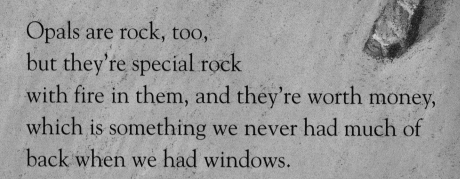

Coober Pedy means
White Man's Hole in the Ground.
In Coober Pedy, we all live in holes
and look for opals—
my dad in the proper mine ...

…and me in the rock piles,
where kids hunt for shiny opal bits
the miners missed.

I'm hoping I'll find an opal good enough to sell,
so I'll have money when we go to Adelaide,
where Granddad and Grandma live
in their house with real glass windows.

I wanted to stay with them
instead of coming to Coober Pedy,
but Dad said they've no money
for feeding someone growing.
And no spare bed.

I like finding opals,
even the bits of them
that aren't worth anything.

When you stare into one,
you see colors—
colors you don't see anywhere else in Coober Pedy.
It's like all the bright green and purple and red
that we ought to have out here
got trapped inside rock.

Now they leave town on ladies' fingers
or stuck in city men's ties.

But there're always more opals.
And when I think I can't stand being here,
not one day longer,
I find a piece of opal and look into it
deeper and deeper:
it's a little like looking out a window.

Then I go help Aunt Grace.
Today she's baking hot cross buns.
"You're just in time, Jean,"
she says, and opens the oven
to take out the first batch.

Her face is damp from the hot stove,
and when she stoops over,
her glasses slide ... off.
They tumble down in the dark space by the wall.

"Bother!" she says.
I kneel and reach for them—they aren't broken.

Then I see something gleam down there,
just where the baseboard would be
if this were a real house.

I get a torch from the cupboard
and shine the light
on the rock.

"Look!" I tell Aunt Grace.
She puts on her glasses
and we look.

Aunt Grace calls for Uncle Peter.
He pulls out the stove,
bends close,
and whistles."Well," he says,
"that's *some* opal!"

Then he finds an old pick
and we peck the opal loose.
It goes a long ways back in the wall,
but finally it comes out—
a big one!

Aunt Grace says this happens sometimes in Coober Pedy.
"But not in my house!" she adds.
I can tell she thinks it means bad housekeeping
to have an opal in your wall and not know it.

"I'd bet your Aunt Grace has scrubbed away a good bit of wall
to get at that opal," says Uncle Peter.

I think that makes Aunt Grace feel better.

Aunt Grace says it is my opal.
But Dad says it isn't.
"We can't accept such a present," he says.

"Don't be ridiculous!" Uncle Peter declares.
"Jean found it. It's hers!"

I'm glad Dad decides not to be ridiculous.

I think I'll sell the opal.
But then I decide I won't.
I put it in a matchbox in my drawer
until the day we go to Adelaide.

All the way down the long, straight road to Adelaide,
I sit beside Dad in the truck,
the little box in my pocket.
Finally, we see houses with yards
and pointed roofs
and flower gardens.

Then we are on Granddad and Grandma's street.
It's narrow, and the houses are old,
but Grandma and Granddad are there,
sitting by their roses,
waiting to hug us.

After hugs, I reach in my pocket,
pull out the matchbox,
and hand it to Grandma.
"It's a present," I say.

When she lifts the lid,
her mouth opens like something blooming.
"Jean!" she says, and her eyes shine.

"I've never had anything so lovely."
She holds it up for Granddad to see.
"Look, John, have you ever seen such colors?"

Later, I stare out the window
at all the sun that's slanting in
and at Grandma's roses
and the trees outside, all greener
than anything in Coober Pedy.

I'm glad Grandma's cheeks are pink
and her eyes shine, happy
when she looks at the opal,
but I think that living here
is like living inside an opal—
the biggest, brightest opal there ever was.
I tell Grandma so.

Then she gets this thoughtful look
and nods, and tucks the opal into her purse
and doesn't look at it anymore.

From my bed on the little couch that night,
I hear her and Dad up late talking . . .

. . . and the next day I find out
that opal has turned into schoolbooks
and clothes and a spare bed—
because Grandma and Granddad want me to stay!

"The opal was a lovely present,"
Grandma says.
"But having you here
will be an even better present for me."

Dad promises to write letters
and send funny drawings,
and I promise him
I'll come back to Coober Pedy to visit.
Often.
I will miss him.

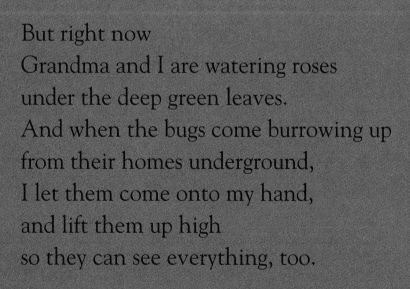

But right now
Grandma and I are watering roses
under the deep green leaves.
And when the bugs come burrowing up
from their homes underground,
I let them come onto my hand,
and lift them up high
so they can see everything, too.